Winter Has Lasted Too Long

James Kavanaugh

Winter Has Lasted Too Long

Illustrations by Edgar Blakeney

A SUNRISE BOOK / E. P. DUTTON / NEW YORK

By James Kavanaugh

A Modern Priest Looks at His Outdated Church
The Birth of God
There Are Men Too Gentle to Live Among Wolves
The Crooked Angel
Between Man and Woman
Will You Be My Friend?
Faces in the City
Celebrate the Sun
America
Sunshine Days and Foggy Nights
Winter Has Lasted Too Long

Library of Congress Cataloging in Publication Data

Kavanaugh, James J
    Winter has lasted too long.

    "A Sunrise book."
    I. Title.
PS3561.A88W55   811'.5'4   76-58865
ISBN: 0-87690-248-4
Published simultaneously in Canada by Clarke, Irwin & Company
Limited, Toronto and Vancouver

10 9 8 7 6 5 4 3 2 1

First Edition

To Those

Who have survived winters past
Who will survive winters yet to come
Who never stop believing
  That flowers will grow!

Introduction

Change and growth are often difficult to measure or even assess. Especially change in the totality of ourselves or the society in which we live. To impatient or superficial observers the dreams of the last two decades have not been realized. There is still poverty, corruption, greed, fear, and violent death.

And yet many of us have changed significantly, and in the depths of ourselves we know we can no longer live a lie. Perhaps this is not a change at all but simply a growing acceptance of what we always knew. Finally we realize that we have had enough—enough of a society that mocks our idealism with specious promises. Enough of pointless jobs, stale marriages, self-serving churches, and fat governments. Enough advice, enough therapy, enough outside answers, enough words!

Women have known enough plastic men and men have met enough seductive women. Enough inflation, enough unions, enough entrepreneurs and other thieves, enough glib liberalism, enough repression. We no longer look to leaders for answers. We no longer believe that any institution will solve our problems.

Thus we have taken our lives into our own hands. Not as naïvely as before, but with a new sense of ourselves. We want more freedom than a country can give, more spirituality than churches offer, more challenge than businesses provide, more love than marriages have produced. We are as revolutionary as we ever were, only more determined and confident. We are still angry at the institutions we have permitted to emerge, and our seeming silence does not mean consent.

We have lived through the complacency of the fifties, the hopes of the sixties, the lies and fears of the seventies. We are ashamed that an oil embargo could frighten us into submission, that inflation could make us slaves again, that conservatism's ebb could blind us to ongoing revolution.

Winter has lasted too long!

It is not enough to provide a better world for our children. We want a better life for ourselves. We are weary of programs, promises, words. We are more ready to live the way we talk than ever before. If we must leave home, we will. If we must risk our lives, we will. If we must live in loneliness, we are finally strong enough. If we still want love, and we do, we know we shall find it.

We will live more simply than before and not be as easily trapped by the trivia that made us slaves. We are not content with the assorted circuses of the space age. We will not settle down or grow up, we will not get serious or stop laughing. We will not conform or take life as it is said to be.

If life can be no other way, we will discover it. We will not be told. We can hear only those whose life matches their speech. We can be friends only with those who listen and understand pain. We will not be forced to accept, to endure, to submit. We will not struggle to possess the weeds of affluence or power. We shall be as free as we want, as mad as we are, as honest as we can. We shall accept no price for our integrity.

There is no need to organize since our community already walks the streets and peoples the countryside in increasing numbers. Yet we know that courage counts more than crowds—a courage that pours from hearts strong enough to live with any pain except deceit. We will continue to talk back to governments, churches, schools, businesses, husbands, wives, parents, experts. We will never lose hope.

We will only die when there is nothing beautiful anymore. Then we shall die in the effort to prevent the corruption of life. If need be, we will reposition the planets and rearrange the stars. We will break the ice with our own hands and water the flowers with our own blood.

Winter has lasted too long!

Yet we recognize how deeply we have been wounded by the institutions that shaped us. We have been corrupted by the greed of business, the complacency of government, the arrogance of churches, the insulation of families, and the compromise of our prophets. No longer! We will confront any president, battle all popes, challenge any power until we can begin to honor a new country, a true God, a genuine love.

There have been no consistent heroes because each is seduced by his own power. We are now content to be our own heroes, preferring love to comfort, freedom to affluence, honest and creative fulfillment to eminence. The sun and sky are beauty enough, life excitement enough, freedom and love the only gifts that matter.

Our dreams may be slow of incarnation, but we will not waste another day. Finally we have a direction, and if it proves unsatisfying, we will find within ourselves the new direction we need. This book is about that direction, not the systematic whole or a doctrinaire escape from pain. It is a heart's recognition that truth matters and love is attainable. It is a fierce promise that Spring will begin tomorrow, because

Winter has lasted too long.

JAMES KAVANAUGH

San Francisco
Spring of 1977

Winter Has Lasted Too Long

Winter has lasted too long,
    Some dullness refusing to leave.
The nights are too sudden for song,
    The days are too cold to breathe,
Gray branches are staring at me,
    Erasing the memory of Spring,
And we have forgotten the song
    A hummingbird taught us to sing.

Winter has lasted too long,
    The river's too frozen to run.
The sky's a monotonous song
    And daffodils groan for the sun.
We stare at the shivering ground—
    We used to make love in the snow.
Winter has lasted too long!
    I wonder if flowers can grow?

Winter has lasted too long!
    We used to make love in the snow.
Winter has lasted too long!
    I wonder if flowers can grow?

The Young Grow Younger

The young grow younger every day,
While I have little left to say.
A lonely bird now says it all,
Or winter gnawing at the feet of Fall.
I did not die when suddenly you went away,
And I survived the night to see the day.
No answers left, no word to end the pain;
Instead, unvaried wisdom of the rain,
Where time is time and life is breath,
Another Spring will rise to silence death,
While I have little left to say,
And the young grow younger every day.
The naked trees bend stubbornly against the sod,
To say enough of life, perhaps of God.
No gurus left, no prophets yet remain;
Instead, unvaried wisdom of the rain,
Where time is time and life is breath,
Another Spring will rise to silence death,
While I have little left to say,
And the young grow younger every day.

Maybe Planets Make the Difference

Maybe planets make the difference
And the stars control the earth,
Maybe all the things I wanted
Were decided at my birth.
Maybe nothing could be different,
Even love was just a game.
And no matter how I did it,
It would all turn out the same.

Maybe Virgo made me cautious.
Did Uranus bring me fame?
Maybe Venus made me love you,
Or should Aries take the blame?
Maybe Jupiter disturbed you,
Maybe Leo made me fight.
Maybe Mercury exploded,
But—where was Mars last Friday night?

If it's all been decided by the stars,
Why have I struggled so?
If it's only the position of Mars,
Why was I the last to know?

The Earthquake Cottage

One day I found a cottage in a garden,
Afterthought of an April earthquake,
   Built by a city's carpenters
When the poor had no other place to rest their heads.
The kind of cottage poets dream about,
   That children and lovers understand.
So I paid her ransom to the realtors
And planned to dress and renovate the land,
   To robe her delicately as a bride
   Enshrined and guarded like a treasure,
   To set her carefully aside,
   Hidden from the world for my pleasure
   To rub away the aches of the day
     With time to listen and play like children.
She was never far from my mind,
   Each scar and wrinkle entwined in plans
     And promises of healing.
She was not beautiful before we met,
   Neglected and forlorn, her joints sighing,
   Delapidated and worn, her heart dying,
Her hands too feeble to brush away the rain.
Too many memories of earthquake victims
Sifting through the rubble to find their children,
Gazing in gaping holes to find courage to begin again.
   Of course she groaned in the wind,
   She had lived through lifetimes,
     Known half a century of wars,
     Saw stock markets fall and immigrants scorned,
     Watched hungry children begging the stones for bread.
     Saw people too poor and weak to eulogize their dead,
     Witnessed the life and death of a dozen presidents,
     Chronicled the hurts and fears of a million residents

Of a city which rose from ashes to survive
And loved just long enough to stay alive
When the journals of the world proclaimed her dead.
This cottage was the city's symbol when citizens cared enough
To build shelter for the poor and homeless,
When religion for a time was more than a word
And morality not a list of sins to be cured.
Of course, she should be cast aside
To make room for the elegant monuments of pride
Which scorn modesty, simplicity, and age
And tear from history books each page of yesterday.
She is not as comely as the lofty apartments which surround her
Nor is she as proud.
But she tells of a time when men were more important
Than legalities—when there was only time
For the realities of shelter and survival.

She is not as dour as time and neglect have made her,
She has known joy as well, from the moment a team of horses
Led her from the compound,
Carried her like a queen in a wooden wagon,
To rest in a garden at the edge of a small hill.
She saw wars end and soldiers return,
She saw wounds mend and poor men earn
The right to feed and clothe their children.
She knew men and women who did not guard their boundaries
Like aliens with walls and fences,
Who did not make a mountainside of inches,
Nor substitute lawyers and arbiters for themselves.
There were quarrels, doubtless, and disputes as well,
But she had lived through poverty and hell,
And learned a bit of life.

She shall be a bride again, though I must dress her
As the culture demands, lest she be laughed at and destroyed.

The fashions are more demanding now,
   The times more complex and less forgiving.
But she shall be a bride again; this nuptial
   Is built upon our mutual, quite desperate need.
   I need her simplicity and memories, her gentle ways,
   I need to know my neighbors without the overlays
      Of advocates and hate. To open up my gate
      In hope that man can care for man.
And she needs me as well, to know that after all the years
   Of living since the April earthquake,
Man has lived long enough to love this widow from another time
   Who brings with her the melody and rhyme
   When all of life depended on each part.

   She shall be a bride again,
   It is the firm decree of fate,
   For she heard the earthquake's warning
   That the hour is growing late.

The Lion Grows Slowly Captive

The lion grows slowly captive in stockade,
His ancient majesty concealed by barricades.
That roar's no more a warning to be feared
Since jungle scars have almost disappeared,
And once-mysterious eyes are only mirrors
While unfamiliar voices crowd his ears.
   This heart was once too young to be afraid,
   His spirit too unbridled to be made
      A lion in a cage
      Where even rage
   Becomes a petulance against the flies
   And gaping children's shrill, tormenting cries.
There's not a decent mountain left to climb,
Nor trembling, baby antelopes to find.
He bathes and drinks in moulded water holes
And vitamins are brought in pewter bowls.
   Hardly a vestige of courage and pride . . .
   Better he stayed in the jungle—and died.

Death! I Despise You!

Death! I despise you!
  Tonight you went too far and killed my gentle friend
  Like a bullying and secret scavenger of men,
  And only timid eulogy will toast your power.
  We could not know the fated day or final hour
  When you would still a loving heart in pointless rage
  And close his eyes as if to turn the final page
  Of a novel read for your amusement at his death
  While bony fingers choked his agonizing breath.
    I promise you this night a cold, unending fight
    Will be the only epitaph I'll live to write
      For my departed friend.

Death! I despise you!
  The single enemy who walks unscathed from wars
  Without a tear, and settles every human score
  With coward's treachery that no one can resist
  Until you add another number to your list
  And twist a face I loved into a chalky shell,
  While I can only curse your shadow into hell
  Until I leave this life without your wrinkled hand
  And die without the pale deference you demand.
    Nor will I dance your dance or feel your clammy touch
    Until I've had the chance to hate you just as much
      As I have loved my friend.

I Took the Train to Work

I took the train to work
    And had my coffee.
I answered the phone at work
    And had my lunch.
I watched a girl at work
    And had a drink.
I caught the train from work
    And ate my dinner.
Tomorrow I will go to work again.
    What's on TV?

There Must Be an Easier Way

There must be an easier way
   To go about living.
      Some stone decalogue hidden at the roots of a tree,
      Some white-haired wise man at the crest of a hill,
      Some hoarse voice whispering in a dark confessional.
I always end up in the woods
   Making gentle love with a sycamore tree,
   Or telling funny stories to chipmunks,
   Or tracing my fingers across nipples of moss.
      —And taking advice only from the wind.

Eddie Potts

Eddie Potts likes straight sex
About two times a week
Unless he works overtime.
The national average is 3.2.
He also likes gravy bread,
Rutabaga and potato salad,
Rice pudding and orange marmalade.
74.8 percent of the nation doesn't.
He's moved once every four years
Excluding a two-year period
When he moved eleven times.
He is in the bottom 10 percent of stable livers.
He's 5'9, weighs 162 pounds,
Has all but four of his own teeth,
And his erect penis is $6\frac{1}{4}$ inches.
He is 14 percent below the national average.
He makes about $11,000.00 a year
Which is $1500.00 less than he spends
And he eats out four times a week.
This puts him 8 percent below the median.
Yesterday he blew his head off
In the basement of his suburban home
Which is 16 percent smaller than the norm.
Only 63 people had done that this year
In towns of 40,000 or less.

Communication's In

Communication's in,
Erasing mortal sin
With conversation games and subtle blames,
And the conjuring of spirits,
By less unfriendly names.

   Beelzebub is finished,
   The devil got his due.
   My guilt will be diminished,
   If I can talk to you.

Communication's in,
Effacing mortal sin
With escalating lips and verbal trips,
And the honoring of angels
By shooting from the hips.

   Beelzebub is finished,
   So tell me what you feel.
   My guilt will be diminished
   With words at every meal.

Little Boy, Afraid of School

Little boy, afraid of school,
Trees and ladders to climb,
And color carefully within the lines.
Not a baby anymore.
The cries in the night lure
No longer the sudden response.
Already freedom disappears
And months are melting into years.
Teachers' voices and divine decrees,
Only moments to linger in the trees.
Dressed and ready now
With matching colors and tailored hair,
And hardly time enough to breathe the air
Of yesterday's freedom.
   When it's all wrong with the world
   Children become husbands
   And dreamers are content to find a way
   Only to own the edges of the day,
   And what the others offer of the night.

Tonight My Loneliness

Tonight my loneliness is very slow to mend
And courage deserts me when such loneliness descends.
I see the shadows on the face I've grown to love,
The eyes that never learned to hide the sudden fears,
And trembling lips that stumble on the rim of tears.
Some deep, abiding numbness settles in my cheeks
As I recall the other lonely walks of other lonely weeks.

My God! I want to stay, to feel the way I felt at other times
In gentle days of silences we shared, the fragile lines
Of hope that bound us even as this darkness now surrounds us.
I hate the pointless words that argue with our souls!
The truth is already bared, these strange syllables we speak
Are but a curse upon the sacredness we shared.
Why must I be alone? Can no one love without destroying
The frail integrity we had painfully struggled to preserve?

What would you have me do? Stand like a soldier and serve
Until some forgiving voice dismisses me as guiltless?
How does one walk away, what is there to say that will not
Mar the healing? Yet, I love you! Do you never understand?
The very fragrance of your body near at hand returns
Without respect for distance or this lonely passing.
We were meant to be children together, drifting in and out
Of each other's lives, not immobilized as husbands and wives,
And thus destroying the very fragile bond that bound us.

It was no bond at all, but some subtle motion of the heart
That could not stay apart without exploring, only doomed
When measured time and others' definitions made it boring
And sucked away the deepest life we saved for our adoring.
Who will ever hear and love me thus again?

For we were more than lovers, the deepest friends
Beyond sex and crowds and in cosmic contact with the clouds
Until the rote demands and ritual hands arose to choke us.

Tonight I barely want to live and even the feeble spark
That forbids me take away my life is but a pale creation,
A faint, unsteady light denying roots or destination.
I am cut adrift, helpless to find my way back to anything.
Too lonely to walk another evening crawling over yesterday
And watching the same dull eyes turn away from my intruding.
This is the loneliness which is very slow to mend—
And courage deserts me when such loneliness descends.

I Saw Your Dreams Die

I saw your dreams die
And felt your silent pain,
Knowing that your child's smile
   Would never be the same.
But what does it matter?
It was only a child's smile
That had to go away,
   So I could love you
     The way I do today.

I saw your dreams die
And heard the silent screams,
Knowing that your vanished hopes
   Were never what they seemed.
But what does it matter?
It was only a child's hope
That died along the way,
   So I could love you
     The way I do today.

There will be new dreams
   Replacing those that fell apart,
     For life is never what it seems.
There will be new hope
   To mend a child's broken heart,
     For love is made of broken dreams.

To Save the City

There is an integrity deep within some few persons
   That will seldom be noticed or clearly acknowledged,
   An honesty more demanding than any ethic
      Enacted by lawgivers or preached by prophets,
   Touching the very reaches of one's own being
      Without regard for education or station in life,
   Although it is likely impossible for the rich and powerful.
   It is beyond guilt and bribery, beyond pain or sacrifice,
   Totally incorruptible under any circumstance or pretense.
Such morality cannot be computed as its own reward,
   In fact, so to classify it would be to corrupt it.
It is perhaps the only eminence a man can truly attain,
   The single masterpiece ever created in man's honor,
   More beautiful than mother with child or any lovers—
      Unless such integrity is the root of their friendship.
It is the single source of hope in the world beyond survival.
   The Socialist has not profoundly believed in man's dignity,
   Nor have Communists sincerely accepted his equality.
   Christianity is a history of enslavement and arrogance
   And Judaism another form of idolatrous self-indulgence,
   Transforming, like the rest, a noble dream into pettiness.

The integrity of which I speak is beyond cult and culture,
As possible and available to the slave as to the free,
Requiring no prophets, since each is already aware of it.
   To call it conscience would be to degrade it,
   To call it a decalogue would be to corrupt it,
   To call it anything would surely be to qualify it.
When it is embraced, it forbids a man or woman
   Ever to lie or dissimulate or be untrue again.

To know one who possesses such integrity is to know God.

To have such for a friend is to make sense of life.
To be such is the only reason I can fathom to live.
　There is no tragedy I can imagine as more tragic
　Than once to have a vision of the purity I describe
　　And out of cowardice or ambition to desecrate it.
The ancients, we are told, called such a pitiable one unjust,
And Abraham sought in vain to find ten not so afflicted.
　The search continues, for it has been decided
　　That only such can save the city.

One More Hill

I've carried lots of people on my back
And climbed a hill or two without complaint.
I've tried to lift a weaker brother's pack,
And walk that extra mile without restraint.
   But lately I've been moving kind of slow,
   And one more hill's as far as I can go.

I've tried my best to heal another's pain,
I've broken bread with many hungry men.
I've covered lots of brothers in the rain
And given more than I've received from them.
   But lately I've been moving kind of slow,
   And one more hill's as far as I can go.

I've tried to think of other people first,
I'm grateful for whatever I've achieved.
I've never been afraid to share my purse,
I'm conscious of the things I have received.
   But lately I've been moving kind of slow,
   And one more hill's as far as I can go.
   One more hill's as far as I can go.

To Patty Hearst

You were the victim of a dream
    To live simply and honestly without power
    To know a love that looked beyond titles
    To escape the boredom of too many things.
You were the victim of a plot
    To destroy the rich in the name of the poor
    To create freedom with rhetoric and violence
    To live by the sword and thus to die.
You were the victim of a drama
    To sell newspapers in bitter irony
    To sate the anger of the resentful and deprived
    To entertain a nation grown weary of its days.

You are an unlikely heroine,
    No Joan of Arc or Mary, Queen of Scots,
    Hardly Heloïse or Lady Jane Grey,
    Just a lonely symbol of a most confusing day.

Does it help to know that some of us don't care about
    The SLA or details of sexual assaults,
    The wealth of your parents or personal faults,
    Solemn judges and self-righteous jurists,
    With one eye on justice and the other on tourists?
Does it help to know that we won't
    Ask you another question
    Or opinion,
    Or look for any sign of repentance?
We are content to know you tried to live another way,
And hope you find a little peace today.

The Zebra Murders:
Black Man-White Man

Your blackness frightens me
On angry nights in silent cities
   When the streetlights illumine my whiteness,
   Pale and iridescent and by centuries accused.
I hear your feet behind me like the drums of your ancestors
   Announcing war on the slimy slave-masters
     Who stole your children.
Hate them, not the feebleness of me!
   You will break down my door in open war,
   Beat me on the streets in cold revenge,
   Stab me with a sword I hoped to use in your defense.
And when I lie dying, you will still live
   As the indentured slave of your own memories.

You are too angry for me, black man,
Too cunning and devious for my schoolbook naïveté,
As evil as I am, as greedy, as loath to admit defeat.
   Your face a mask of darkness hiding desperation,
   Your smile a weapon to wreak my desolation.
     Your nose broad and unforgiving,
     Your lips thick with ancient bruises,
     Your eyes dark pools of resentment,
     Your skin frozen like an onyx angel
       Heralding some impending sorrow.

I am too frightened tonight to be your friend,
   Afraid of your scars and savagery,
   Afraid of your silence and vengeance,
   Afraid of your chitlins and ribs,

Afraid of your smells and laughter
   And the mad monotony of your music.

No order of God or government can change what time has done!
   I am not the moon's master or sultan of the sun.
   I am the stars' victim as helplessly as you.
   When you bid me undo what I never did, you ask me
      To ride on clouds and corral them on the horizon.
You have made white beautiful and powerful
   And master of your destiny.
I have only lived with it, unaware of its color.

I am not ready to hold your hand, only to walk closer,
   To see a little better than before.
Perhaps our children can be friends, or theirs.
I have hurt you too much, but you have hurt me as well
   With your facile lies and accusing eyes and arrogant cries
      Of "Black is beautiful!"
White is beautiful as well, and feeble!
White is lonely as well, and frightened!
White is victim as well, and weary!
   Love your blackness as best you can
   And I will love my whiteness
      More tenderly than before,
Until the snow will settle softly on the blackness
   Of mountain rocks,
And frame in ermine beauty the edges
   Of a dark and rushing mountain stream.

I Want to Die a Careless Man

I want to die a careless man
   With my yellow legal pages scattered on the floor,
My desk covered with ashes and unfinished thoughts,
   Borne away on the wind of an idea,
   Not far from one who loves me
     And understands enough of my madness
     To stay until the end.
I have not learned much of life,
Each evening a new mystery to wonder about,
   Struggling somehow to stay alive
   Among so many satisfied to survive.
Tonight I have no time for prophets or profit margins,
   I do not worry about the failure of socialism,
   Or the vandalism on buses after school.
   Nor do I care what the President thinks.
I would like to watch a flock of ducks
   Circle a swamp three times before landing,
   Eavesdrop on coyotes at the edge of a forest,
   And hear church bells across a quiet valley.
Most of all I would like to die a careless man.

I Met Death Today in Sunlight

I met death today in sunlight,
  Smiling softly like a flickering candle.
I'd seen him formerly in dark disguise
  And peering monk-like from the edges of the night.
A spectre lurking in surprise and leering in the morning light.
    Those dusty knuckles knocking at my door,
    That groaning deep within myself,
    An eerie creaking underneath my floor,
    A silent stare when lust had spent itself.

I met death today in sunlight,
  Smiling softly like a flickering candle.
A man no stronger than myself
  Who craved the friendship I withdrew
With misplaced dreams and fantasies of wealth.
    He stood as naked as the breeze,
    Not cursing or confronting me in fright,
    As eager now to talk with me
    As I was loath to see him in the light.

I met death today in sunlight,
  Smiling softly like a flickering candle.
No hermit with a lantern,
  No shriveled prophet with a scythe,
Only a child grown older with soft and understanding eyes.
    "Life is long enough," he said.
    "Yesterday will not return."
    "Love will come again," he said.
    "Tomorrow's time enough to learn!"

Jack Kildaire Died Last Night

Jack Kildaire died last night
And honest tears accompanied him to the judgment seat of God.
In an unprecedented move by heavenly standards
He was permitted to bring one person
To the august and fearful confrontation.
Knowing Jack, who had sued 137 times in an active life
And been countersued 84 times,
It was not surprising that he chose his lawyer.
His accountant was rumored to be upset but realized
That although Jack had earned 11 million dollars
In forty active years, he had spent 4.7 million on attornies.

After some deliberation by the lawyer
On proper attire for the divine court—
He selected a soft gray pinstripe and black velour vest—
The awesome drama began!
Jack swore on St. Peter's beard—the Bible had not been used since the
    Reformation—and hardly had uttered the words
When his lawyer demanded a change of venue, which was denied.
There were two weeks spent in jury selection (the voir dire obviously
    being unlimited),
Since Jack was a rich, white Presbyterian who employed wetbacks and
    no women,
Except in a massage parlor in which he held a 40 percent interest.
He openly despised gays, Jews, blacks, teamsters, Russians, and
    Mexicans who understood English.

The trial was going well into the sixth week
When Jack's widow complained that legal fees had swallowed the
    insurance money
And forced an only daughter out of college.
The lawyer agreed to accept the family home and car,

Which he graciously leased back to Mrs. Kildaire at 2½ percent
    under market value.
Jack himself signed a lucrative contract with a New York publisher
And pledged all royalties to the legal firm which defended him.
After the usual threats of mistrial, perjury, and invasions of privacy,
The jury was out for three weeks—complaining consistently about the
    bad food and the harps at night.
Ultimately the jury was unequivocally hung, Jack and his lawyer embraced,
    the widow moved in with her sister,
And Jack was sentenced to eternity in Limbo, where
He sat in a straight-back chair looking at a white wall for all eternity.

His lawyer returned to earth, collected 1.7 million in fees,
Made the cover of *Time* magazine, divorced his wife,
Retired to the lecture circuit, lived in Jack's home,
And a year later married his only daughter.
At the wedding ceremony he toasted his bride with humble, eloquent words:
    "I owe it all to Jack!"

Making Too Much of Life

Making too much of life
    Like it won't come around again.
Leaving it round-shouldered and limping
    With too much weight on its ankles.
        Demanding what it may never do.
        Waiting for what may never be.
        Missing the eagles gathered on the corner,
        And cursing the pigeons instead.
Who said life should do it all?
    Love every moment, peace beyond words,
    A friend who finally understands?
Life is a mystery man
    Making few promises, stumbling in and out,
    As generous in chance as in careful plans.
Death to the architects and calculating builders
    Who lay foundations!
Life is no building, no subtle blueprint.
    It is as unpredictable as clouds,
    As forgetful as spring rains,
    Hardly impressed with equality or justice or truth,
    Willing to ignore my faults and failures
        . . . if I am.

Someone Lied

Someone lied!
  I knew it as a child.
Man never left the ocean,
   Lulled to sleep by motion of the tides
    He hides beneath peninsulas of sand
And fears to walk upright upon the land.
   Content as hermit crabs to dwell
    In someone else's empty shell,
  He crawls within his secret den
    Until he needs a home again.

A Song to a Little Boy

Little boy, with so much living to do,
How much truth should I pass on to you?
 Shall I tell you of my fears
 That increase with passing years?
 Shall I talk about the love that disappears?
 Should I talk about the pain
 That I've lived my life in vain?
 Shall I tell you of the dreams that end in tears?

 Shall I talk about the day
 When my childhood passed away?
 Shall I tell you of the many times I strayed?
 Should I talk about the time
 That I almost lost my mind?
 Shall I talk about the dues that I have paid?

Little boy, with so much living to do,
How much truth should I pass on to you?
 I will tell you of the joy
 Just to know a little boy.
 I will tell you of the value of a friend.
 And no matter what you give,
 To be free is all there is,
 And I'll tell you of a love that never ends.

Hilda

Well, it's obvious to anyone, Hilda,
That our love can no longer endure.
Even I must admit that we're not right for each other.
After all, six months of great sex and a lot of laughs
   Isn't everything,
And certainly not enough on which to build
   A lasting relationship—
As all the approved authors seem to say,
   Especially since you seem to have found
     A more fulfilling companion.

I'll just disappear now, Hilda, without hostility.
   I can lose!
If, however, some night when you are loving him,
   And he is pleasuring you in a very special way,
Should you accidentally call him by my name,
   Would you write?

It Is in the Mornings

It is in the mornings
I miss you most of all,
Before the day begins,
When the sun hesitates
And the gray skies argue quietly
Before the dawn,
When last night's dream fragments
Leave me wordless and helpless
In some childhood hiding place
And old tears wait too patiently.
The evenings are seldom long
And sleep comes soon enough
To ward off disappointments
And the shattered pieces of the day.
It is in the mornings
I miss you most of all!

Some Walk Through Life

Some walk through life with no monuments
   For anyone to admire.
Not a house built or a child,
   Not a city reconstructed or an apple tree.
Content with some vague freedom.

   There are enough lovers,
      Enough creators and artists,
Not enough who live their own lives
   And walk strong against the sky
      Without murdering or expecting,
      Calculating or dissecting,
Just drifting along without plans.
No noble causes or sudden losses,
   No wise words or sprawling herds,
Ready to die along some dusty street,
   If so it must be.
Some ego centered deep inside
   And a rare appreciation for life
Without clever definitions or subtle ambitions.
Knowing
   That there are enough trees and clever men,
   That it's time to clear the land and walk hand in hand
      With life,
      Going nowhere,
      Content
      Withal
      To be.

Tonight I Am a Lonely Tree

Tonight I am a lonely tree
Who will not endure another winter.
Spring! You made such promises!
And now I sit in silence
Unwilling to feel another gust of wind.
Water flows freely in the rivers
And thirsty roots drink therein.
I am not thirsty anymore, dry and lonely,
Afraid of the ambitious forests where
Strong tree fights to rise above strong tree.
I will remain in this quiet grove,
A twig unheralded and ignored,
Without leaves to fall each autumn,
Without buds to break my bark
And with it, my heart.
Do not water me with words!
Do not fertilize me with love!
Do not prune me with cleverness!
Leave me alone, sheltered from the wind,
Without shape or hope,
Without destiny or promises.
For tonight, I am a lonely tree
Who will not endure another winter.

It Hurt

It hurt
When Mother reminded me
Of the Christmas Play
I starred in as a child
Because I knew
My brother had played the part.

It also hurt
When my lover reminded me
Of the great night we had
When I wore my silk pajamas
Because I knew
I never owned any silk pajamas.

I wish to hell
I had been
In that Christmas Play.
I would have been dynamite!

How Much Love I Wasted

How much love I wasted on those I never loved,
How much time spent in motion with a motionless heart,
  Listening to the words
    which only echoed in the clouds,
  Hoping to make amends
    for what I never did.

How much love I wasted on those I never loved,
Longing to be alone with my dreams,
  Fearing to walk away
    from barnacles of childhood,
  Promising to return
    when I had never been there at all.

Once I Smiled

Once I smiled like a summer breeze
Even in winter,
Until the seasons of my life
Were as monotonous
As the soft clouds and blue skies
Of Hawaii and the Caribbean.
I was a travel bureau
Denying rain and hurricane,
Apologizing for the sudden storms
That came rarely.

Now a menacing cloud
Can interrupt the placid days,
A lashing wind awakens palm trees
And covers the beach with flotsam.
The sea leaps before me
And tourists take cover in grass huts.
Lights dim and radios rasp,
The birds pull in their wings
And the heavens open up
In unrelenting deluge.

Then there is quiet after the storm,
The birds return to tease the tourists,
And my smile is as warm and real
As the gentle, cleansing rain.

I Haven't Seen the Sky for Days

I haven't seen the sky for days
Nor felt the sun on my face.
I am as pale and troubled
As the weary ones I wrote about,
Severed from myself by shadows of compromise
Where sycophants whisper of empty dreams
And love is lost in tired schemes of cleverness.
Traps are everywhere to capture birds in nets,
Rope more obvious, fine silk too subtle to detect.
Cookies and milk can make me prisoner!
God! I hope there is time for one wounded in childhood,
   Time to leave and be free,
   Time to greet myself each morning,
   And at night to love what I see.
I am falling apart like an old wall
Crumbling in twilight at midday,
Begging comfort from the shadows,
Still concerned with what the shadows say,
And I haven't see the sky for days!

One Day I Saw a Lonely Mountain

One day I saw a lonely mountain
Rising up to touch the edges of a cloud.
Its scarred face softly purple in the light,
Its strength unacclaimed but unmistakable
While the cloud floated there in soft surrender
With a memory of the seasons it had survived.
There were no words to mark this gentle union,
No nuptials echoing down the valley below,
No promise of warmth or coolness in the shadows,
Only the unhesitating act of this natural embrace.
Even the sun was silent as they slowly kissed
Without obvious passion or dramatic display.
I wondered how long the mountain had waited,
Knowing the cloud would appear when it was time,
And what ancient stories it must have whispered
When the cloud brushed her fingers across his jagged face.
He had known other clouds which only closed his eyes
And separated him from the sprawling valley below,
Wrapping him in a shroud of loneliness and confusion
Until this moment when the patient planets were all in place
And enough seasons had sculpted his body in sun and snow.
It was as loving a moment as I had ever seen
When a lonely mountain made a silent cloud his queen.

You Have Joined the Gray Rocks

You have joined the gray rocks and cannot hurt me now.
Your face lost in a mountain landscape, your color gone,
Your features blown blank by a nameless wind.
   Once you were as warm as a woodfire in a forest cabin,
   As familiar as the smell of baked apples.
   We were children together, slept side by side,
   Feared the creaking phantoms of the night,
   Dreamed of firecrackers and beebee guns,
   Crossed frozen swamps hand in hand on fragile ice,
   Watched the nervous beavers with hushed voices.
      Maybe it was the beavers I loved,
      Their whiskers wet against rising waters,
      Noses twitching in the wind to search out enemies.
When did our hearts turn cold as the air?
When were we only the shadows of spruce trees?
Now we will be strangers till death, nodding at funerals.
   The landscape grows larger with age,
   The twilight more intense,
   The sunlight more solitary.
I remember a skinny boy laughing in the snow.
Tell me it was not you
   So I can dream of him tonight.

Fastidious Ladies

Fastidious ladies buying new drapes
And carpets to match, telling the doctors
And interior designers what husbands will never know.
Neglected bodies re-covering the couch,
Planning to re-cover themselves.
Maybe he will look again, maybe he will notice.
Sexless lives draped in velour and fine satin,
Sexless wives carpeted in wool and clever nylon.
Styles take the place of love.
Too late to find a cottage in a garden
And a man who needs tending.
Too late to feel the pressure of his presence
And a heart that needs mending.
Nothing to walk to, no one to talk to,
Stale words echoing off deftly colored walls.
Sameness settled in like a burglar alarm
To keep out intruders like pain and real laughter.

I Started My Own Business

I started my own business
  Fortified with loans and pride
As excited as a middle-aged groom
  With a young and blossoming bride.
I told my former employers at APPLEBY & SON
That I would never again endure their tantrums
  And the unbridled use of my name.

The stationery was embossed with my title
Displayed proudly in the center
    About ten minutes before the salesmen entered
    To salute my new venture with copy machines
      Before there was anything to copy,
    And business forms before I had any business.
There were health plans for selective liars,
Christmas gifts for prospective buyers.
    How did the Chamber of Commerce root me out?
Alarm systems, fire extinguishers, bookkeeping aids,
  Coffee machines, answering services, ad displays,
Water coolers, furniture leasers, postage meters,
  Uniforms, detergents and electric heaters.
      Hire a woman, a cripple, a black,
      And just when I started to relax
The Feds demanded my withholding tax,
  Followed by the State and County
  And a recently enacted bounty
    On sprinkling systems,
Whereby I paid the PUC for theoretical water
  Just in case I had a fire.

Then there was workmen's compensation

And two weeks of paid vacation,
    But for an office boy?
The unions wanted TV in the lounge and separate latrines
And the Health Department called about my soap machines.
    And the secretary I hired for martini luncheons
    Joined a commune with my aging accountant.

I started my own business—there must be something I lack.
    Today I called Bill Appleby,
        And Monday—I'll be back!

I Am Strong, You Know

I am strong, you know,
Tried by experts,
Left lonely on bare floors
And hated by those who loved me.
Nights of sadness have not taken away my life,
Nor days of melancholy and madness.
I am a quiet cave hidden in ocean rocks,
A fir tree watching giant redwoods rot away,
A patch of grass at the edge of a roaring river,
A stone that has known the desert's heat
And survived till the sun was gone.

I am strong, you know,
Oppressed by tyrants,
Abandoned on dark nights
And cursed by those who praised me.
Winter's raging has not bowed my head,
Nor years of loneliness and aging.
I am a silent spring trickling down the mountain,
A patch of snow refusing to melt,
A patient crack in granite rocks,
A tree that was bent at birth
But has not fallen in the cold wind.

I am strong, you know,
Some kind of man has somehow grown.
I like the strength that lovers give,
But I am strong enough alone.

David at Auschwitz

David knows how many bodies
   Were piled at Auschwitz,
How many noble men destroyed
   And loving women violated.
He has seen all the movies
   And read all the books.
He donates to Israel generously
   And returns there periodically
To marvel at the pioneer spirit
   And gather news of more atrocities.
He never talks of Arabs.

David also lives in a large house
   On a high hill,
Runs a powerful corporation
   His grandfather built,
And graduated from Harvard Business School
   With outstanding honors.
Last year he made two hundred thousand
   Buying and selling cheap apartments.
He celebrated Hanukkah
   And paid no taxes.
He never talks of tenants.

   Today at lunch I told David
      He was as racist and elitist as anyone else.
   He told me I was anti-Semitic.
Neither of us ate dessert.

Drinking Free with Muhammad Ali

I was having drinks the other night
Right after a heavyweight fight
With a couple of entrepreneurs and skillful doers
   Of damn near everything financial.
The one guy with a thin nose admitted
   That he divided three thousand acres in San Diego
      Into one-half-acre parcels
And made almost two million dollars.
The other guy with the fat cheeks was hardly impressed
   And acknowledged that he bought and sold
      Eighty apartment units in L.A.
And made a million in ten months.
The television announcer said that Muhammad Ali
   Got a hundred thousand for every minute he fought,
Which seemed to impress the thin nose and the fat cheeks.
   It was at this point that I admitted
   I won ninety dollars playing keno in Reno
      On a twelve-dollar investment.
I also bought their drinks.

Of Young and Old

The young men talk of victories,
    The frightened of failures.
Old men laugh quietly
    Or say nothing at all.
There is nothing as tragic
    As a young man who seldom smiles
Or an old man
    Who has too many words.

Each Day Comes like the One Before

Each day comes like the one before
With ever-mounting responsibilities
Until I know that I am not happy,
Working to eat like all the rest.
And what does it matter, the quality of the food,
The shape of the space, the size of the chair?
Today no more than yesterday and then tomorrow.
I will climb a mountain soon, or build one,
I will follow rivers soon, or dig one.
It is sad to let the days lead me,
Each running its course, colliding with the next.

I was destined to be a strange old man
Living in a small forest but not far from friends,
Where I could write of gophers in the sun
And shy deer standing in the meadow,
Where I could hear the rustling plants
Growing in the wind and note the buds on trees.
I was a wandering, curious child made to conform,
Transformed and made to serve another's lost childhood,
And then to have another child to recover mine.
I am a small man asked to think big.
Such is the most terrible curse of all,
For death comes too soon!

Soft Touching

Soft touching and gentle embraces
Are latterly barely in vogue,
Supplanted by transplanted orgasms
And assorted chasms
Of hormones about to explode.
When I was younger
And apparently less hormonal
There was a lady who used to come around the mountain—
When she'd come.
Lately I've wondered what happened
When she didn't come.
Probably rode those big white horses
Till she did.
My friend Dooley Davidson
Got eleven women off 107 times
And only came twice himself.
That's gotta be self-sacrifice.

The Night Was Once My Friend

The night was once my friend,
More gentle and understanding than the day,
    With time to talk of memories and old scars,
    With time to wonder about yesterday and tomorrow.
Now we are silent,
Our friendship turned to formality
    Of a restless bed and voiceless darkness.
The night comes and goes like some phantom lover
Who promised a moment's ecstasy before the dawn came
    To lure her away with traffic sounds
        And children off to school.
Once there was twilight,
    The softening of the rocks,
    The hills reduced to silence,
    A deer cautious at the edge of a canyon,
    The creaking of crickets finally attended,
    The voice of the wind soft and unscolding.
Now there is day merging into night,
And night hungrily rushing into day.

What kind of man is this
    Who has lost friendship with the darkness?
    Who has transformed night into an empty tunnel
        Between the days?
I need once more the gentle strokes of twilight,
And thus again to make the night my friend.

Twelve Thousand Miles

Now you may thrive on a Sunday drive
And weekdays take the bus,
But it won't be long till your warranty's gone,
    And your auto bites the dust.

    Twelve thousand miles—or a year—whichever comes first.
    Twelve thousand miles—or a year—whichever comes first.

Your car works well for a hell of a spell,
Until your warranty's gone,
Then a little bug hidden under a plug
    Jumps out to sing his song:

    Twelve thousand miles—or a year—whichever comes first.
    Twelve thousand miles—or a year—whichever comes first.

If your car burns oil or you need a coil,
It's when the warranty's dead,
On that very day when you pull away,
    Remember what was said:

    Twelve thousand miles—or a year—whichever comes first.
    Twelve thousand miles—or a year—whichever comes first.

Well, I settled my score with the auto store,
I took the man for a ride,
When I dropped him there in the desert air,
    "How far is town?" he cried.

    Twelve thousand miles—or a year—whichever comes first.
    Twelve thousand miles—or a year—whichever comes first.

Where Has Passion Gone?

Where has passion gone?
The hungry love that cannot wait for darkness?
The desperate love that ignores the moon?
The love too impulsive to light the candles?
    Sweating in the back seat of cars,
    Panting and groveling on all fours,
    Rolling across wet lawns and hard floors,
    Making a warm bed of damp leaves and dried acorns.
Passion did not go away, only freedom.
No one loves like a free man!
    But when he cannot endure the pain
    He finds a mother again
        To provide order and clean sheets,
        Healing and well-balanced meals,
        Comfort and respectable dreams,
And to take passion away!

Suburban Marriages

Suburban marriages
    Don't look so silly tonight.
Maybe boredom beats this kind of pain.
Maybe they understand that people just kind of hang on
    And call it love.
Maybe they're the wise ones,
    Not ripping at life and tearing at the seams,
    Not pulling out the stitches until it screams.
But meanwhile,
    I'll have another go at it.
    I think you're lurking out there
    Somewhere
    And we won't have to do a lot of philosophizing!

Love But a Part of It All

Love but a part of it all
Better left unsaid.
Who gave currency to words beyond wonder?
Love is more spontaneous than God,
Beyond compare with yesterday,
Beyond charts and words and graduation.
My love is a tenuous thing,
Fragile and afraid,
Crowded easily,
Less significant than freedom.
I would rather be free and useless
Than well loved and made prisoner.
Loneliness will not destroy me,
Not for now at least.
Only servitude—even of love.

You Close In on Me

You close in on me like a gray day
Suffocating the love just beginning to breathe.
I am no houseplant panting for biweekly water,
Stretching my dull leaves for a touch of sun.
I have love to give, the kind that lasts
Longer than late movies and perfume commercials.
Your presence loves me as much as I need.
Is there no place for gentle kisses anymore?
Is there no love that flows like rivers
    Only cresting and overflowing its bounds
       In flood time
When the mountains unravel their avalanches of snow?
I love our friendship, hate our love,
Love what we do, hate the intervals
    When I must fill the void
    That never can be filled.
Must you stare at me begging for the love you counted on?
    My passion smothered before it burns,
    My lips enveloped before they taste,
    My hands grasped before they touch.
Do you not understand?
    I must possess my body before I can give it away.
The love that satisfies you is a token
    Conjured from any passion available.
Give me room to love, space to be alone,
    Or I will disappear as quietly as I came.

Some Voice Is Calling Again

Some voice is calling again,
  Echoes everywhere.
Dreams of night more explicit
  And terrifying,
And in the day more melancholy
  And troubling.
I know the call, there's no denying it.
I am grateful that it still penetrates
  The deafness of present appetites.
I have rested for a while, hoped to be satisfied
  With the love that ties the rest to freeways.
I am missing some part not available in hardware stores.
  Too much travel to rely on warranty,
  Too much madness to be cured by banalities.
I hear the laughter on the streets,
  Watch them rushing to the parks on holidays,
   Feel the torpor of their return,
   Hear the groans they fear to utter.
But most of all I hear the voices, calling, calling,
  Come away to I know not where.
  Echoes, echoes, echoes—everywhere!

Searching for Some Idyllic Peace

Searching for some idyllic peace
   In an empty room,
Not noticing the days that drift by
   Never to return.
What is this elusive hope?
This child's creation
   Of distant landscapes and quiet beaches?

It is only freedom's urging,
   Some vague response to life imprisoned,
   Grown dissatisfied with morning walks
     And what's for dinner,
   Hardly content with financial victories
     And tokens of success.

I will pass on such love for now,
My pain is too deep for routine strokes.
   Meanwhile love will come along when it comes,
     A child's sudden smile,
     A gentle lady in the afternoon,
     Conversation till dawn.

I need to walk unfettered,
   Aware that my own needs
     Are as unique as I am,
   Aware that I can never find peace
On the paths of another's dreams.

The Writer

The writer makes coffee in his room
    Waiting to greet the morning alone.
Free to shave if there's a reason,
Seldom bothering to make his bed,
Ignoring what the headlines say,
And hearing the silences instead.

    Not an office to go to
    Or a servant to bring the mail,
    Not an order to give
    Or a stranger to ring the bell.

    A solitary spokesman,
    A middle-aged charade,
    Unthreatening as sunlight
    And sometimes in the evening afraid.

    Wondering if he's done anything
    Save sing forgotten songs,
    Hearing only church bells ring
    Till evening comes along.

Lonely man is only man,
He knows it best of all.
Armed with only feebleness
He hears some distant call.

    The writer makes coffee in his room,
    Waiting to greet the morning alone.

Raised Poor

You can always tell a rich man
   Who was raised poor.
He drives a Lincoln
   and runs out of razor blades,
He has a big house
   and the bristles are matted in his toothbrush,
He has a freezer full of steaks
   and makes everyone clean up his plate,
He buys new suits
   and keeps the old one,
He has money in the bank,
   and knows it will disappear tomorrow.

After the Divorce

Little boy, hating mama's lover, hiding under covers,
   Knowing that your daddy won't be here.
Little boy, fighting mama's lover, crying to your mother,
   Shedding lots of crocodile tears.
Your daddy isn't coming home again, so you hate
   Instead of living with the pain.

Little boy, hating mama's lover, hiding under covers,
   Soon you'll have your mama all alone.
Little boy, fighting mama's lover, clinging to your mother,
   How you gonna keep your mama home?
You see your daddy's got another lover, too,
   So I'm about as good as you can do.

Little boy, weeping to your mother,
   Gonna throw a tantrum every time.
Little boy, sleeping with your mother,
   Life is not another nursery rhyme.
You better find another game to play,
Or you'll drive your mama's lover far away!
   Your daddy's got another lover, too.
   And I'm about as good as you can do.
      I'm about as good as you can do.

The Secret Love Affair

It started as a secret love affair
   In dark motels and trysts along the beach.
No words can match the passion of that pair,
    And heaven only knows the heights they reached.
      She hung on every syllable he'd speak,
      He kissed until her starving lips were raw.
      They only had a couple nights a week,
      Until they turned their trysting into law.
They married in a church along the bay
   And purified their lives from private sin.
They didn't stay apart a single day,
    Until a growing boredom settled in.
      They fought and sulked and mumbled of divorce,
      They moved apart to purify the air.
      He took a second job, she took a course,
      And twice a week they had a love affair.

Compromising Man

Compromising man, afraid to stand alone!
Trapped in love's demands.
Victim of another's starvation dole
And loath to pay the slave-master
The price of freedom for your own soul.
How long will you postpone life in feebleness?
You are the slave-master!
Biding the time asking questions
Of another Jesus hiding in long robes,
Sliding in line with the vestments
Of a pale Redeemer under every stone.
Begging approval with self-inflicted tears,
And building a passing kingdom of parasitic fears.
Forget the promised land!
Walk from Egypt by your own voice
And make your own covenant in the desert sand.
Hang upon a cross of your own choice
And rise from death by the power of your hand!

To Say Good-bye

I would like to say good-bye with some dignity,
Not to calculate and bide my time
When another's fantasies arose to swallow mine
Until I heard myself repeating unfamiliar dreams.
I am the single enemy of my freedom,
Love's prisoner, requesting permission
For what is already mine.
So now I begin again, guarding against
The subtle bonds that only tie my hands and feet.
My heart was never bound, only anesthetized and waiting.
My strength is shy and tardy to appear,
Content to compromise a year—to survive.
Then I am finally alive, laughing in the light
And wondering how I survived the night.
Does anyone ever learn?

Wandering Man

Wandering man,
   Time to settle down and die,
   Time to heed the warnings of the world,
   Time to hear the tailored jailers with the key of life.
Walls fold their arms before you,
Clocks clench their fists,
Phones scream like burglar alarms,
Romance curdles in kind words,
Even the banker shakes his index finger.
No place to run anymore
   When another's weakness is stronger than your intent.
No time for fun anymore,
   When a wandering man comes home to pay the rent.

The Revolution Has Arrived

The revolution has arrived
   And the poor will take their vengeance everywhere.
The dirt farmers fighting for an acre
   Will do battle with the greedy developers.
The shirtmakers teaching their children to sew
   Will rip the clothes from the tailored businessmen.
The mothers whose babies scream for milk
   Will tear at the breasts of elegant ladies.
The fathers whose sons were sold to slavery
   Will hang the masters with their children's chains.
     Patience is almost at an end,
     Only leaders are lacking.
   They will climb hills and break down doors,
   March on neighborhoods and invade the stores,
While cultured voices grow suddenly hysterical
   And once proud eyes will know what terror is.
The leisured class will return from island vacations
   And take up arms to protect their children.
The token programs are too late, yesterday's promises unfulfilled.
   The Socialist dream is but a scholar's compromise,
   And Democracy an inflammatory word that has lost its dignity.
The revolution has arrived
   And only a fool would not see the signs.
   The dying have nothing to lose but their lives.
Race will battle race, poverty and oppression will unite,
   And finally men will understand their root community
     In the common color of flowing blood!

A Phantom of a Man

A phantom of a man
   Covered with the trappings of masculinity,
Some vital integrity,
   Lost in childhood and never to be regained.
Some decay at the root of your seed.
A thief without courage to steal
   Save from the IRS and petty cash.
A kissing Judas
   Who hides in the shadow of dying trees.
The history of perversion:
   Gambling with another's love,
   Creating war to conceal treachery,
   Infiltrating with conniving alliances,
Wanting what brave men have, but too weak to die with honesty.

No man respects you, even your specious ally.
Others will use you as you have used them
   Until you are useless.
What do I care? All you take from me are trivia
   You could have had for the asking.
You are the world's auctioneer,
   The last object for sale is himself,
Until all,
Finally,
Is gone.

An Angry Old Man

An angry old man with no one to be angry at,
    Muttering to silences,
    Cursing shadows,
    Mumbling over sidewalks,
    Stumbling over curbs,
    Battling noises and fighting voices.
Love is finally forgotten.
No dreams of long hair and full breasts
Or silent walks along the sea.
    Silence is dangerous,
    Rage is master now,
    Sealing the familiar sounds
    With headstones
    Snatched from graveyards everywhere.
Death will call him soon,
As defeated and alone as the snarling dog
Who snaps at him as he passes.

One wonders if love ever had a chance,
Or if, like the ocean, each wave
    Was propelled by yet another wave.
Perhaps I will snarl back at him tonight
    To let him know he has been heard
    By other than dogs
And thus to love him.

Why Do I Sit Lingering Here?

Why do I sit lingering here,
A mature man of intelligence and zest,
Scarcely sipping my malingering beer,
Just to see the profile of her breasts?
I could approach her glandular beauty . . .
With the charm I can muster off duty . . .
But she would probably turn petulant.

Her breasts are too pushy not to notice,
Challenging the sun on white beaches,
Succulent to see like ripe peaches,
Guiding me into dark bars,
Sliding me into parked cars.
She never had to make the football team.
Enough to walk across the street!

What must it be like to have eyes devour you every day?
"Tedious," she'd say. "Repulsive, animalistic, obscene!"
She shoulda followed me today, I spent a month not being seen.
No breathing appendages leaving strong men breathless.
Does she know how she frightens me?
Breasts bulging from sweaters, breasts bending to serve,
Round ones, oval ones, the pointed ones that curve.
Fat ones, flat ones, the kind that test the dress,
Added ones, padded ones, the kind that make you guess.
Wobbling, wiggling, throbbing, giggling!
Now I ask you, "What kind of man sits lingering here?"
"Er . . . bartender, maybe one more malingering beer!"

My Happily Married Friend

Tonight I invited my happily married friend to dinner
   And sought his mature advice
      About my troubled relationship.
    I recalled in some detail with honest pathos
      The depths of my ongoing love,
      The hint of self-destruction,
      The struggle of time together and days apart,
      The strain of commitment and my divided heart.
    I sincerely wanted to reach some decision
      Before this collision of wills destroyed me.
After a shrimp cocktail and a decent chicken cacciatore,
   He comforted me with the details of his own story.
   Midway through dessert he had described his entire life,
   And in the midst of a superb brandy,
     He decided to leave his wife.

Big Sky Heat

Big sky heat goes through me,
I am as gold as the rimrock,
Brown but not dusty,
My shoulders sloping against the horizon,
Sweating my way to freedom,
Watching the dirty river grow fat,
Watching the children swim in the public pool.
God, I love the frontier faces here,
Patient eyes that know the rains will go away.
Strong, honest faces that don't say the unnecessary.
What has happened to the cities?
Sophistication covering the lust and lustre
Of strong bodies and open eyes.
Someday I'll buy a wagon
Pulled by a pair of fat oxen,
Grab a frontier girl and head for the hills,
With no thought of where we're going,
And no mind to where we've been!

Is There No End to Childhood?

When will I cease to be a child
Giving an accounting of every day,
Watching my dreams defiled,
Asking another's permission to play
And bidding someone else's God good-night?

Some louder voices always there
Stealing the silence from the dawn,
Following my footsteps everywhere,
Creeping stealthily across the lawn
And surprising me in the bushes.

Childhood has too long endured,
Praying for empty relatives,
Mouthing only proper words,
Doing what no one else forbids
And telling the truth in silence.

Is there no end to childhood
When everyone's opinion counted
Except my own?

He Is Older Now, Yet Not Peaceful

He is older now, yet not peaceful.
 Successful days are only distant memories
 When younger men relate their present victories.
  "It's different now," he says in repartee.
  Afraid to say, "It frightens me!"
Who will tell us of life? Whom can we believe?
Is there no wisdom save in alcohol's reprieve?
 But, God! Assuredly he's free to boast,
 He served his time and made the most
  Of what he had.
 Another drink and he'll recall it all,
 Reclimb the peaks that time has rendered tall
  Until tomorrow.
Then sadness will return to kill,
When he will be older still,
 And yet not peaceful.

There Is Some Disease

There is some disease afoot among men,
Some savagery beyond quieting.
No pyramid of gods can calm it,
No cant or chant or promises of eternal life.
Men kill so easily, sell one another's souls,
Rise on the ashes of friends,
Grinding once-loved bones to compost.
Who has not killed or been killed?
Who has not felt the burst of rage
That sends a murderer to his own hell?
I have long pondered this savagery,
Dreamed that another century would exorcize it,
Struggled that it would take leave of my own heart.
I know that systems of morality are frightened men's prisons,
That the gods are only empty idols fingerprinted by the hands that
    fashioned them,
That healers go unheeded and prophets die untaught.
Is there no hope?
I do not know.

Sometimes there is in the morning
When I take time to see the skies.
Sometimes in the evening,
When a gentle light rises in your eyes.

Indian Maiden

Indian maiden with firefly eyes
   Dancing in the dark,
I see you in moonlight,
   Your face soft against the bark of trees.
A fragile body beneath my strength.
   Some secret never told,
     Waiting to love me.
Helpless cries in the night like a wounded rabbit.
   Silent after love,
   Restrained, not devouring,
   A softly bubbling spring washing the rocks,
   Waiting for the dawn under animal skins,
     Warm against my legs.
Too much tenderness for passion,
Surprised by your own appetite,
   Hands softly losing control,
   Mouth fixing on fingers and toes,
     Gone mad beyond words.
Then silent, silent, silent,
   In hushed respect for love,
     Surprised, surprised by love!

There Is a Love

There is a love beyond all boundaries and rational intent,
A love that is not so much a free act as a collision in space,
That will leave father or mother, yea child, to be with its beloved.
   It is a helpless love blindly transformed into madness
   And tolerates no critics regardless of experience.
Every other love is soon replaceable by time and circumstance,
And the pain at its passing will with diversion disappear.
For even the pain is but a hunger for a lost attention
And not the soul-rooted cry of a dying animal begging for food
Or a careening planet pleading for some liberating orbit.

In the presence of this love, far beyond lust or even friendship,
Options dissolve and the cautious rules of normal expectations
   Are severed in a single, knowing glance.
Such love is rare, and appears without regard for age or merit.
   One must seize upon it nor fear to ask too much
Owing to the gathered guilt or false nobility of lesser loves.
If such love, soon or finally, makes some cautious compromise,
It is then reduced to the laws and banalities of every other love.
Once gone, it will not reappear without great suffering, if at all.
To have known it even briefly is a rare privilege, and when gone,
   The most acute pain ensues at its demise.

Such love is the folly of those who must ask everything of life,
The unsettled and dreamers, the searching, distant ones
Who cannot put their deepest feelings into the poverty of words.
   When it is gone, the wounded lovers will pass from love to love
   Without dismissing the hope that the beloved will reappear
Even then one wonders if the uncharted pillage can again occur.
A month of such love is worth a lifetime of the rest, not for most,
But for the rare few who can detect reality from clever sham,

Manipulation from utter madness, consideration from a soul's lust,
And are born with such painful vision and spiritual appetites
That no other love or any obstacle can impede its quest.

Such love adds little to the good order or government of the world.
It only establishes that beyond the routine paths of most lives
There lurks an unknown God Who calls those mad enough to understand.
    Such a God places more value on this love
        Than on life itself,
    For all things are by fortune and energy attainable
        Except this love!

I Am Your Frightened Lover

I am your frightened lover
Afraid of yesterday's pain
And the steady rain of memories.
Once I groveled fearfully,
Called a name tearfully in the night
And pleaded like a child for the light,
Begged for a mother's love.
Who made us man to want a mother?
Who built us thus to need another's undivided love?

I am your frightened lover
Longing for some refined
And yet undefined freedom.
To feel release from the locked jaws
And clutching claws of our own fears.
The choice is such a futile one,
To love and watch courage disappear
Like some bald and simpering Samson,
Or not to love and feel only the strength
Of some recurring loneliness.

Somehow loving is so final,
Some judgment cast to make all the morrows predictable,
A coward's gasp to make spontaneous love respectable.
When winter nights have come too soon,
Will familiar and wrinkling lips still quiver?
When harvest clouds conceal the moon,
Will there still be a fawn at the twilight river?

You Grow on Me

You grow on me
Like the yard I played in
With the peach tree in the rear.
You grow on me
Like the grass I layed in
In the spring of every year.

You grow on me
Like the field I strayed in
When the sun had chased the snow.
You grow on me
Like the creek I played in
In a spring so long ago.

Flowers grow where flowers can
And birds know when to sing.
My love for you can still renew
That memory of spring!

I Will Hold You Softly Tonight

I will hold you softly tonight,
Hoping that our togetherness
Will not take away my strength.
Some night I will collapse in your arms,
Let my manhood tumble around me,
Let my gathered strength fall where it will
Like the weight of a dying warrior.
Do you not understand why it is hard to love you?
Tomorrow I must face them again
   Who can laugh and hurt me,
   Tear at my flesh,
   Crush the proudness of my chest.
I would give you the single key to my energy,
Threaten to dissipate the strength I found
To tear away from my mother's breast.
I was so slowly weaned
And would have you nurse me once again,
To stroke my head and tell me all will be well,
That my words are not foolish, my fears unfounded.
But tonight, I must content myself
To hold you softly,
Until I am more certain of my strength!

Your Face

Your face more gentle now
That summer's gone,
The sun and sadness
Do not stay as long.
Some silence settled in,
Some deeper peace
That heeds the winds
And eerie flights of geese.
The shorter days
Content with softer light,
Nor quarrel with
The coming of the night.
I do not miss
The suddenness of dawn,
Your face more gentle now
That summer's gone!

I Have Only Dusty Love

I have only dusty love
But I would have loved you had you waited.
All the things you cried for would have been yours
Had you not climbed the walls of night
    To preview the dawn.
The moon and stars were light enough,
A patch of neon along a lonely highway.
You wanted sunlight! You demanded it,
    Created it from bonfires and jelly beans,
Circled yourself in headlights and luminous eyes,
Until those eyes were no longer mountain lakes
    That cast my reflection so unmistakably,
But screams of discontent and who will pay the rent.

    I am no apostle of love.
        I am its least likely advocate.
        The pain in my stomach is caution,
        My lips are parched in protest,
        My eyes glance obliquely lest I see too soon.
    I am a child of Endor,
        Black as night and running from the day,
        Virgins in sunlight frighten me away.
    No one with reason still intact could love me.
Only a woman as mad and scarred as I,
    Who somehow sees a dusty love
        Across a summer sky!

Life Has Its Beginnings

Life has its beginnings
Coming at intervals,
Time to start anew.
None is first or last,
Save birth and death,
Nor can we decide
Which is most significant,
Transforming, or long enduring.
It only matters that
Each beginning, like spring,
Be given its due:
    To nourish the earth
      for flowers,
    To respect sun and rain
      for fertility,
    Not to trample feeble life,
      our own or another's,
Before it is strong enough
    To bend in the wind!

There Are No Perfect People

So now you know my secrets, the little things I do,
  The quiet nights I'm hurting,
  The days I laughed with you.
The fears that never happen, the dreams that never end,
  We cannot know the future,
  But I will be your friend.

There are no perfect people,
We're old enough to know,
So stay around to love me,
And watch the rivers flow.

You know the words unspoken, the angry words I've said,
  The gentle words of loving,
  The breakfasts served in bed,
The days I couldn't make it, the scars that wouldn't mend,
  But nothing really matters,
  If you will be my friend.

We've known the pain of loving,
We've known the quiet glow,
I'll stay around to love you,
And watch the flowers grow.

The days are getting shorter, the nights are not so long,
  But we are still together,
  And time has made us strong.
There are no perfect people, we're old enough to know,
  But we are still together,
  To watch the flowers grow!